Stories

for

Upside-Down

People

Right-Side-Up Stories
volume One
For Upside-Down People

Written by

Melea J. Brock

Edited by Marcia Coppess

Design & Illustration by Karen Newe

Published by Right-Side-Up Stories

Melea J. Brock
Right-Side-Up Stories
260 South Lake Avenue #185
Pasadena, CA 91101

All scripture quoted in this book is from
The Message © 1993 by Eugene H. Peterson.
Used by permission of the
Nav Press Publishing Group.

All stories in this book have been
published previously in other form.

Library of Congress
Card Catalogue Number: 98-96713
ISBN 0-9667455-0-7

There is an eye-to-eye,
ear-to-ear, heart-to-heart
kind of intimacy with a story.
Anything can happen
in those short moments
where you and I meet...
anything.

These stories are dedicated
to storytellers young and old,
naïve and wise.
May you find the heart
of the Story and tell it
with all of your heart.

Contents

How to Use This Book

Read this book to others aloud. These stories have always been oral stories. Read them to children and friends and family members. Nothing would please me more.

It's okay if you feel a little rusty with your storytelling. Did you know that we love to hear the familiar voice? It's your voice the listener wants to hear, so use it. And when you tell these stories to children, please remember that they sometimes have questions (right in the middle of a story). They love to talk about a story. Let them talk. You will learn something you never expected to learn. What you have set up to be a special teaching moment for them just might end up being yours.

Read these stories for your own enjoyment. Let the stories ask you questions. Let the stories have lots of "shelf life," which simply means to give them the time to find a place in your heart and your head.

When we read a story, we bring all of our history, our emotions, our hopes and dreams and ambitions . . . we bring us! In fact, try to lay aside your appraisal of these stories so that they can speak all the way through to your middle. Let God whisper to the deepest needs and hopes and dreams of your heart. He has done that for me with these stories and I am sure He will do the same for you, my friend.

Use these stories in your classrooms, Bible studies and Sunday Schools. They already have been used this way through my story tapes.

Here are some questions that might prompt open-ended answers and discussion—

- *Which person did you identify with the most in the story? Why?*

- *What do you think might have happened next in this story?*

- *Did the story touch on something you'd never thought about before?*

◆ *What would you like to do about what this story is saying to you?*

Use this book if you're a pastor. Dear pastor, you have my permission to use this book for your sermon illustrations or whenever you want to raise one of these stories to your church family. I don't have to tell you that you are following The Great Storyteller each time you lift a Truth about Him through Story. I ask only that you note my authorship and direct people back to this book.

If you'd like to use this story for the purpose of public performance in a school, church, community gathering, etc., I ask that you please seek my written permission first by contacting me *(see About Right-Side-Up Stories* on page 91.).

Enjoy!

Step Inside

There's something
about a story for me.
A special invitation
to come away.
Shhhh...be quiet.
Crawl upon a lap.

It's as if the world
stops spinning 'round,
and the day's troubles
take a nap.

And I make a choice to listen,
to the secret something
bound and wound in lines
and pictures there.
Oh, yes!
There is something
about a story,
if I allow its words to woo,
to tickle, tease, poke and
prod the Me within the Who.
"The Who?" you ask.
Well, it's the Who I think I am.
The Who I long to be,
the Who that's hidden
way down deep,
the Who that's really Me.

So step inside
this place with me,
it's ours for just a blink.
A place for you and me to sit,
to feel, to think.

Perhaps somewhere
within a story,
we'll take a step or two,
look back and see
our footprints—
Our Me within the Who!

Mary Alice
Bennett's
Box

his story is about

me and you.

A story about

hearing God speak

to the deepest

questions, wonderings

and ponderings of

our hearts.

any will tell you God doesn't speak to people anymore. I don't think that's true. And you'll never convince Mary Alice Bennett of this, for she will sit you down and tell you this story.

Mary Alice was always a wondering, pondering, questioning child. She asked questions all the time. Questions about weather and countries and animals and insects and rocks and trees and people and food and cars and planes. Her parents bought her "Tell Me Why" books, but they didn't always tell her why. They bought encyclopedias, but the encyclopedias had missed many of her subjects. They even bought a bigger radio. But still Mary Alice Bennett had unanswered questions.

Then, sometime during the summer of the ninth year of her life, Someone started answering her questions, kind of out loud, in her head and her heart. She found that if she was listening really hard, like Mrs. Harding in the first grade always made them do, she heard a voice . . . a still, small voice. She figured this voice had to be God's. It was strong and yet kind, honest and truthful. And the voice always called her by name.

In fact, God's voice began with a box. The head counselor at the summer camp that year had put a box out on the craft table the first day and told the kids that God cared about every question, every need they had. There was a slit in the top and they were supposed to put their questions inside. She never saw the box move from that craft table and the sides were taped shut, but God answered one of her toughest questions that summer. So when she got home she started her own box. She saved every unanswered question, every wondering, every pondering in a little cardboard box. She'd write each question down on a piece of newsprint paper in the teeniest and tiniest of writing. Then when the answer came, she'd turn it over and write it down on the other side.

And she found that over time she had to flatten and push out the sides of her box to make it bigger. It wasn't very hard, for she was very good with scissors and glue. The box changed its boxy shape and over time it lost its shape altogether. Oh, but this didn't matter to her, for inside this funny-shaped container was the treasure of the world. There were answers about things like—Why do humans need sleep? Where do clouds come from? Do we live on the top of the world or the bottom? How come humans don't have tails if they have a tailbone? When does a person become a grown-up? Why is there hate? If when you are sad, you feel blue—then what color is love or anger or happiness? And then, the saddest question she'd ever put in the box: Why did Grandpa have to die?

Over time, she grew up and her shape changed too. And sometimes her question box would sit high on the top closet shelf. After all, "One must not be too serious," she would say to herself inside. But late at night or on the most lonely of days or even when she was feeling fine, she'd pull the box down and spill its contents onto her bed and think and ponder and puzzle.

She loved to stack up all the answered ones—there were hundreds of them. The others she spread out in little columns on the bed. Some were on fresh white bits of paper written in her sophisticated teenage penmanship with little circles over all the places where a dot should be. Questions like—When do boys grow up? Will I marry? Where should I go to college? What will I do with my life? How old do you have to be before people listen to you? And sometimes, she wondered if God heard her questions, and sometimes, she wondered if He cared about her and her box. He seemed silent at times. It was hard to listen; it was hard to hear Him when everyone else in the world talked so loudly.

Time went by and the box moved wherever she moved. From home to college to apartment after apartment and finally to her very own home. Anyone else would have taken one look at this misshapened mass of cardboard, tape, glue and string and tossed it out immediately. Not Mary Alice Bennett. It was still the treasure of the world to her. The funny shaped cardboard box had shaped her life. God had kept right on answering through the years. Sometimes before she had even asked. It was as if He knew her questions already. She'd write them down anyway. It was good to have a record, a history, a memory.

In her thirties though, a depression, a darkness swept over her life. It was not any one thing that caused it, but a series of events that, when all added up, left her feeling bruised and empty and sad. Day and night she poured out her questions to God. Day and night, she pondered morbid thoughts. Nothing seemed to help. No one seemed to understand. The voice of God became distant to her. And finally she decided God had stopped speaking. He didn't speak to people, really—especially people like her. And so, she reasoned, she had made up the whole thing about God and the box. So, she took that box and shoved it to the very farthest part of a dark cupboard that she never used. And with the box went Mary Alice's hope.

She could only hang on to her work now. She'd get up, go to work, come home and cry, cry, cry. She shut herself off from family and friends and stopped the newspapers, the phone, the mail. "I will not speak to anyone and no one will ever speak to me again."

Then one night, after weeping for a very long time, she fell asleep. She had a very strange dream about the box. She dreamed that she died and went to Heaven in her pajamas with that funny-shaped container tucked under her arm. To her surprise, God was glad to see her. He put his arms around her and held her closer than she'd ever been held before. "I'm so

glad you're finally here Mary Alice. Come . . .
come sit with me and let's have a look at your
box. I've been trying to answer your questions.
Have you heard me?"

She could only stare back at Him with
tears streaming down her face. So this is what
God really looks like. He was huge and robed
in the color of the sun. The hair on His head,
face and arms was snow white. His face was
fatherly. It looked old and young all at the
same time. His eyes danced and sparkled like
that of a child's. And His voice was as she
always had heard it—strong and yet kind, honest and truthful—the way she had heard it all
her life.

"It doesn't matter anymore," said God.
"I have all the time we need to answer your questions. Shall we begin?" He pulled Mary Alice
Bennett close to His side and she placed the box
on His lap. "It's beautiful!" God whispered. She
could hardly see the box through the tears flood-
ing her eyes, but she knew its shape. She untied
the lid and together they began to search for the
first question.

They talked and laughed for hours,
punctuated with quiet moments of silence and
serious understanding. It was very comfortable in

Heaven. The clouds were as soft as she had always imagined. And the angels who drifted by over their heads waved knowingly to her, and to God, of course.

There was only one question left in the box. She handed God a yellowed scrap of paper. It read: "Why did Grandpa have to die?" God paused and whispered to an angel sitting nearby.

God turned back to Mary Alice, "Would you like to ask Grandpa? It was one of the first questions he asked me."

Her heart started to pound. "Grandpa's here? But I didn't think . . . ."

"Oh my, Heaven's never been the same since your Grandpa arrived."

The memories flooded back. Grandpa had a very playful side as grandpas go. He played hide and seek, read to her, always kissed her on her forehead and let her pat his bald head. He taught her how to tap dance and how to play horseshoes and checkers.

Just then her eyes saw someone walking toward her and God. He was still bald and a little round and still Grandpa. The minute he saw her he started running and when he reached her, he swept her up into his arms and hugged and kissed her—just as he always had.

"Oh, Grandpa, I've missed you. Look, I'm all grown up now."

He smiled proudly. "Yes you are." His eyes began to change and the corners of his lips began to quiver as if he was going to cry.

"Grandpa?"

God put his hand on Grandpa's shoulder, "Go ahead, tell her."

Grandpa nodded his head in agreement and took Mary Alice's hands in his. "I was sick for many years and never told anyone. When I did, the doctors told me it was too late. I'm sorry for the time we lost. But you, Mary Alice Bennett, are the reason I'm here in Heaven. If God could answer a little pig-tailed tomboy's questions from a box, then maybe He could answer the ones I'd had all my life. So for days in that hospital bed, I asked 'em all and He answered."

He was holding her hands very tightly. "Mary Alice Bennett, don't you give up!"

"What? What are you talking about Grandpa? I'm going to stay here with you now."

"No, it's not time. You're going to have grandchildren, Mary! Don't you give up." He was now speaking fast and with a certain desperation. "Their names will be Holly, Katie and Daniel. You're going to play hide and seek with them, teach them how to play checkers, bake cookies and they're going to fall in love with you, because you'll be their grandma."

Now Mary Alice was crying. Grandpa knew everything. "And you're going to teach them all about God, because they're going to have little funny shaped cardboard boxes like their grandma's. I didn't have time to tell you all I know now. I met God moments before I died—and you still have a lifetime. Go back . . . . "

"How Grandpa?"

"Go back and live it!"

"How? You don't understand. I'm all alone. There's no one left."

Just then, God pulled her close to His side. "I'm here," and He gestured to her head and her heart. "I've always been here, haven't I? And I will never leave you."

Something stirred in her that she remembered feeling at nine while sitting around a camp-fire. An overwhelming confidence, a lightness, a surety about life. She stood up and turned to God and Grandpa. "I've got to go back! I'm going back!" She picked up her box and started walking away backward across the clouds. "Thank you! Thank you! I love you," she shouted. "I love you both so much!"

I bet you know what happened next. Mary Alice Bennett woke up from that dream and ran to that dark cupboard and pulled out an old, dusty cardboard box.

She didn't give up. Her life changed. She became a grandma, eventually. And somewhere in another state there's a wonderful old woman playing checkers and baking cookies with her three grandchildren tonight. She'll tuck them into bed and tell them how soft the clouds are in Heaven, what God looks like, what their great-great-grandpa was like. Then they'll beg to see Grandma's box one more time. She'll smile and walk over to her dresser table and pull out a brittle piece of paper. She'll tell them about how God spoke to her, still speaks to her and how He is just waiting to speak to them.

And some will say it was all a dream or "My, what an imaginative child." And there will always be those who say God doesn't speak to people, but you will never convince Mary Alice Bennett of that. ♦

The Worriers

This story is
fun and very honest.
Come on, we all worry.
Take a deep breath
and hold on to your
W's as you tell!

what if? who? what? when? where? why? well? WOW!

There once was a family . . . a family of five—Walter, Wilda, Walt Jr., Winnie and little Willie Worry. And oh, how they did worry, that is. They had a nice home, nice neighbors, nice jobs, nice schools, but they never really knew it because Walter, Wilda, Walt Jr., Winnie and little Willie Worry were too busy worrying. They were wearisome worriers. Why they could out-worry the best of 'em. In fact, Walter and Wilda came from a long line of worriers. Both their mom's moms and their dad's dads were worriers and rather proud of it. For you see, when you worry you don't make too many mistakes. You're pretty wary of everyone and everything. Wow, could they worry!

They worried about waking up on time. Upon awakening they then worried about the weather. And because of the weather worrying, they wondered when to wash and wax the car and when to wash the windows, because one never knows when the weather's going to take a turn for the worse.

They worried about what they ate and whether what they ate would make them wane and waste away.

They worried about the way-out economy and the rising cost of wax paper, Necco Wafers™, windshield wipers and bottled water. And was it really wise to have your wisdom teeth pulled?

And sometimes, but not often, they worried about the world and whether people in this world would ever grow weary of having their own way. Now, that's pretty noble worrying, if you ask me.

They worried about their neighbors next door—the Websters and their teenage son, Wesley. Walt, Jr. and Wesley were good friends. They were in Mr. Witgenstein's World Civ class and planned to go to West Woonsocket Tech and study word processing where upon graduation they would probably wed two winsome women (one each, of course), buy Wedgwood china, work out at the gym and wait for the big break. But wait, I'm wandering—back to the Websters.

You see, the Websters sometimes took trips

on weekends to visit Grandma Webster who was ill, but still very wiry.

The Worrys worried about Wesley on those weekends. They worried about the cars that came to the Webster's with wiggly, giggly teenagers. And well, why would any parent leave a wahoo kind of teenager all alone to weigh and make weighty decisions? What would he eat? When would he go to bed? Where was he going with all of those friends?

On those weekends when the Websters were away, the Worrys got in a whole week's worth of worrying. They were worn out by Wonday, I mean Monday. But still they felt it was worth the worry because they really cared about Wesley and the Websters.

The Websters were the least of their worries when you added them all up though. There were the three different schools their children attended which averaged several hours of worrying per day. You see, they worried about the education Walt, Jr., Winnie and little Willie were receiving. They worried about the teachers wearing pants—Miss Williams and Mrs. Watson, that is. And would the wearing of pants by Miss Williams and Mrs. Watson affect their children's education?

They worried about Coach Weston and why wasn't he warried, I mean married. After all, he was thirty-three! Yes, he seemed very warm and had a winning way with the Walhabi Walrus Water Polo Team, but what was he waiting for— the perfect woman?

They worried about little things like wasting paper in the classrooms, the wax coating on the milk cartons, watering the football field after the weather had taken a turn for the worse. And whether saving the whatcha-ma-callits from the tops of soda cans would really save the whooping crane from extinction.

They worried and they whined to one another, but they never really wanted to get involved. After all, they weren't sure whether they should make waves about these worrisome issues. Surely some other wonderful parent had worried over these very things and made someone aware. And if not, oh well. One can only do so much worrying.

They worried about their jobs and worker's compensation, withholding taxes and the soap in the washroom.

They worried about their church and why weren't there more willing workers willing to walk the walk *they* walked.

They worried about the city they lived in, Walhabi, Washington—and whether they'd ever have a Dairy Queen™ like the one in Wenatchee, Washington. The one in Wenatchee used real water-processed decaffeinated coffee and real whipped cream in their Blizzard™ shakes.

They worried about the reputation of the great apple state of Washington. You see, they could never ever seem to find those little Winesap apples in the winter and these apples were supposedly available in the winter. Why?

They worried about the United States and warm weather trends from the Mount St. Helen's eruption in 1980. And they worried about preserving the wildlife of these United States such as wild rice, wild oats, wild pansies, wild parsnips, the wild rose and the infamous game of wild pitch baseball.

Their worry even stretched world wide—to the World Wide Web, of course. And the Windsor Castle in England and the Windsor Family and the Windsor chair, the Windsor knot, the Windsor tie and were there more Windsor some-things in this world to worry about besides all the Windsors they already knew about?

And then one day while the Worrys were sitting on their Windsor chairs, having waffles and going over the worries of the day the phone rang. It was God. Wow!

Oh yes, God knew the Worrys. He loved the Worrys. He wanted something wonderful for the Worrys.

You see, he had tried waking them. He had tried whispering to them. He had tried warning them. He had tried whacking them one. Why God had even tried the wire service. God had something to say to the Worrys.

It was going to startle their stingies, flap their unflappables, arouse opportunities, wham their worries. The potential was promising. The possibility for monumental and momentous discovery was waiting to be welcomed by the Worrys.

Well, it was Wilda Worry who picked up the phone that day.

"God?! As in God the Father?" Her voice quivered with worry as she listened. "Yes, God. Walt, Sr. is right here eating his waffles.

"Yes, Walt, Jr., Winnie and little Willie are here too. Put them on the extensions? Right away, God."

Wilda turned to her family whose jaws had dropped wide open and said, "Grab a phone! It's God!"

They didn't walk. They all ran to the nearest

phone and waited and wondered and worried about what God was going to say.

"Yes, God. We're all here," said Walt, Sr.

"Worrys, I want to say something to you. I've been trying to say it to you for a long time." His voice sounded warm, not wild with wrath.

"Yes, God. What is it?" their voices waned a bit.

"My beloved Worrys, are you tired? Worn out? Burned out?"

"Yes," they all said . . . even little Willie.

"Then come to Me. Get away with Me and you'll recover your life. I'll show you how to take a real rest. Walk with Me and work with Me. Watch how I do it. Learn the unforced rhythms of my Grace. I won't lay anything heavy or ill-fitting on you. You keep company with me, my beloved Worrys, and you'll learn to live freely and lightly."

The Worrys had never heard such words before.

"Let me see if I have this right, God," said Walt, Sr. with wonder in his voice. "We give you our worries and you'll give us the peace that passes perception?"

The Worrys couldn't see God smiling on the other end of the phone, but He was.

"Yes," said God, "That's exactly what I want to give you. Peace—my peace."

"Well, speaking on behalf of all the Worrys, God, I think we'd like to walk and work with You! If you're not too busy right now, could You come over for some waffles?"

And God said, "Oh, I've been waiting for you to ask. I'm on my way. In fact, I'll bring the whipped cream!" ♦

The Land of Stinky Feet

his story was
written while I worked
with high school people.
I wanted them to know
how very special they are
in God's kingdom.
I wanted to encourage
their servant's heart.
May it do the same
for you.

There was once a land called "The Land of Stinky Feet," and that is truly what it was once . . . *stinky!* No one seemed to know it, though, for the longest time. In fact, they denied it, lied about it, pretended and ignored. But one young man named Ernest confronted all that. But wait, I'm getting ahead of the story.

The Land of Stinky Feet didn't start out stinky. They say the land smelled of roses and lilacs. When the breeze was just right, people from clear across the valley could smell the wonderful floral fragrances wafting their way from the land. Well, that's because, of course, no one's feet smelled then. Back then, they were footwashers. Yes, footwashers!

You see, a long time ago, a Footwasher

dropped by their land with shiny wash bins, fresh Turkish towels, cakes of soap, lotions and pow- ders. He set up camp by the river. And to their surprise, he didn't seem to be selling anything, just asked to wash a foot or two. Well, that sounded pretty interesting.

His touch was gentle, the soap was creamy, the lotions were soothing. Ingrown toenails, cal- louses and corns—gone! Hammer toes, heel spurs, bunions—healed! Dry, flaky, itchy feet— treated! The gunk between their toes—disap- peared! Sore, aching, tired muscles—massaged!

The people of this land had been taking care of their own feet for years, scrubbing, scrap- ing, medicating. But after the Footwasher, well, nobody had ever experienced these kind of feet. It was amazing! It was wonderful! Their washed feet seemed to change their whole person! Getting your feet washed by the Footwasher was the best part of the whole day!

Orderly lines of young and old alike would begin to form down by the river around seven in the morning, with the last big toe dried about midnight. They spent hours with the Footwasher, fed him well, gave him a little cottage to stay in, and generously paid him for his services.

Then came the dreadful day that no one

had anticipated: the Footwasher announced that he had to move on. "Why? Who will wash our feet like you do?"

"I can show you how," he said with a smile in his eyes. "If each person washes one pair of feet a day, your feet will forever feel wonderful. Come; follow me down to the river and see."

Everyone took part that day, and they were quite excited to find out that it wasn't as hard as they had imagined. Willingness, tender care, and the right footwashing equipment were all that was really necessary. In fact, washing feet was as wonderful as getting one's feet washed. There was such a feeling of helpfulness and accomplishment, and the thank yous fell on the ears so nicely.

Sadly, the day came when, early in the morning, the Footwasher had to leave. Everyone helped him pack up his things and followed him to the edge of town to wave a bittersweet goodbye.

"Remember, ten toes, two arches, two soles a day," he yelled to the crowd with a twinkle in his eyes.

"We will! Ten toes, two arches, two soles a day! Ten toes, two arches, two soles a day . . ." and soon he disappeared over the hills.

Everyone stood there feeling a bit empty and sad 'til the crackly voice of an adolescent spoke up. "Well, let's get started!" It was Ernest, a boy not more than twelve or thirteen. But just the same, each person grabbed their basin, towel, soap, lotion and foot powder and off they went into their day.

Now, the Footwasher had said, "You'll know which pair to wash if you look with your heart instead of your eyes." So that's what they did and the first day went very well indeed. Everyone's feet got washed! It was amazing! Not one single toe had been left untouched, from the tiniest newborn to Old Grandpa Duncan. The next day, same thing: everyone's feet got washed. Next day, same thing: everyone's feet got washed. It was as if they'd been washing feet all their lives. It was a little bit embarrassing when asked, especially if you were new to the land, but your feet felt so splendid after, and the footwasher felt so splendid after, that it was worth the cost of a few pink cheeks.

Some of the best footwashers in the land were the children. They weren't afraid to ask, "Have you had your feet washed today?" And they giggled and chattered and the soap bubbles went everywhere as one received the specialness of a child's touch.

And the older the footwasher, the more

gentle and careful they were with a person's feet. They listened as they washed. They made the owner of the feet feel very important. I think it was the wisdom of age. "After all, you want a pair that'll last a lifetime, don't you?" they'd say.

And life went on and on, day to day—ten toes, two arches, two soles a day.

But, as I said earlier, things changed in this land. You're not going to believe this, but some people lied about having had their feet washed. Footwashers slacked off and said, "I'll wash an extra pair tomorrow." Some decided to hide behind spanking new shoes and fancy socks and stockings. Some preferred certain footwashers to other footwashers. Some made up excuses. "Why don't you go wash my neighbor's feet first?" or "My feet are still clean from yesterday." Some just flat-out refused to wash or be washed!

Well, little by little, an aroma began to fill the land of the footwashers. A smell that was old and stale, like a gym locker that hadn't been cleaned out all year. Like a pair of sneakers that had been worn and worn, but never washed. Worse than Limburger cheese and rotten eggs. The smell grew pungent, acrid, burning to the nostrils, but no one noticed it. Not one person!

As the smell grew, the sound of "Ten toes, two arches, two soles a day" was fading. The little town downwind could hardly take it on a breezy day. And they started calling that land, "The Land of Stinky Feet!" In fact, they kept clothespins in their pockets for just such breezy days.

Ernest was one of the few willing footwashers left in the land. He'd load up his basin, towel and soap along with his books and lunch. He was a senior now and he'd become rather sad and disheartened about footwashing. The daily refusals were almost more than he could bear. Even his parents disagreed with him. "Is footwashing worth all this?" But sometimes he'd get a vision of the Gentle Footwasher. "Ten toes, two arches, two soles a day!" And he'd try again.

Another fall was approaching in The Land of Stinky Feet. Ernest had been accepted to a university on the other side of the valley, and one Indian summer day he loaded up some duffel bags and his VW™ and kissed his mom and dad goodbye. "See you at the break."

"Going to miss you, son!"

"Me, too," said his dad. "But not all the talk and pressure about footwashing."

Ernest drove all day, and by early evening he reached the sleepy college town and stopped at a nearby diner. He sat down at the counter next to a man reading a newspaper.

Soon a waitress appeared with a menu and an aerosol can. "Here you go. Special's meatloaf and do you smell that?"

"Smell what?"

"I don't know, kind of like old gym socks, really old gym socks?" She spritzed the air a few times. "Do you smell it, Doc?" She was referring to the man at the counter next to Ernest as she spritzed the air again. The Doc just looked at Ernest.

"Well, that should take care of it. What'll you have, son? Our cheeseburgers are the best in town!"

"Make it a double cheeseburger, French fries, chocolate malt and a slab of that apple pie a la mode, please."

Ernest sat there drinking his ice water. "Boy, I sure don't smell anything." The gentleman folded his paper and smiled at Ernest as the waitress placed their orders in front of them. "Enjoy, Doc—and you, too, kid."

"Excuse me," said Ernest, reaching across the counter for napkins. "Are you a real doctor?"

"Yes."

"What kind of doctor?"

"I teach at the university here in town."

"Really? I'm a first semester freshman!"

"Well, you won't find a better school for podiatry."

"Podiatry? What's that?"

"The specialized care of feet. In fact, I could take care of that problem of yours in about a half-hour's treatment."

"What problem?"

"Son, your feet stink."

"What?!"

"Your feet smell."

"My feet smell?!"

"Your feet smell. That's what the waitress was complaining about."

"I don't smell it. I really don't smell it!"

"That's the problem with stinky feet. A person doesn't always know they have 'em. When was the last time you changed shoes?"

"These are new shoes!"

"Hmmm. When was the last time someone washed your feet?"

Ernest was silent.

"My office is nearby, son."

On the walk over, Ernest explained the story of the Footwasher and what had happened to their land over the last several years. He couldn't recall the last time someone had washed his feet.

The doctor listened patiently as Ernest poured out his heart. At his office, he soaked, bathed, lotioned and powdered the boy's feet. The touch was so gentle and familiar to Ernest. He looked down at the man crouched before him with the towels over his arms, silver basin flashing. Then it hit Ernest.

The face was older and bearded, and there was a small bald spot on the top of his head, but six years changes a person's looks. His heart started to pound. *Could it be?* The gentle doctor then looked up into the hopeful teenager's face. And Ernest's heart leapt.

The Doctor's eyes smiled and out came those familiar words of long ago, "Remember? Ten toes, two arches, two soles a day."

Ernest remembered. Spontaneous tears poured from his eyes as he stumbled to his feet to hug the Footwasher.

"I knew it was you! All of the sudden, I just knew it was you."

"It's me. It's me, son. Sit down, Ernest." He handed him a fresh pair of cotton socks, sat on a small stool across from Ernest and looked right into his eyes.

"You know, Ernest, I teach a course here, 'Intro to Podiatry.' I think you'd find some answers to what happened to your land. And I know you'll learn more about your own feet."

"I'll take it!"

"Nothing would please me more. Now, remember, ten toes, two arches, two soles a day."

"I will! Ten toes, two arches, two soles a day!"

The phrase hummed in Ernest's head as he walked back to the diner to pick up his car.

When he got there, Ernest discovered an old man sitting at the bus stop in front of his VW™. The old man was looking into Ernest's car and scratching his head.

"Hi," blurted Ernest. "How are you?"

"Pretty good. Your car?"

"Yeah."

"Noticed your towels and basin in there— sure could use a foot-washing."

"What did you say?"

"I said I need my feet washed, son."

It had been a long time since Ernest had washed someone's feet. His hands shook, he got soap in his eyes, but the feeling was exhilarating! It felt wonderful to wash feet again!

"I'm a little out of practice."

"You did great, son. Thanks—thanks for taking the time to wash an old man's toes."

The semester seemed to fly by. The Gentle Footwasher, or "Doc" as the students called him, asked Ernest to dinner the last night of final exams week. The diner was packed, but the two of them found a booth in the very back. Over double cheeseburgers, fries, chocolate malts and apple pie a la mode, the Footwasher said, "Ernest, it's time to go back home and tell them what you've learned."

The thought made Ernest's stomach do a flip flop. "I know. But I don't think anyone's going to listen to a 19-year-old. I feel all alone. I'm scared."

"I know you are, but it's time to tell them about their feet. Who will tell them if you don't?"

And in that moment Ernest caught a glimpse of the future of those he loved. Eternal stinky feet!

"Ernest, they already know about their stinky feet. Somewhere inside, they know. You're ready."

The next morning, Ernest loaded up his VW™ and took off for the Land of Stinky Feet. Miles before he was even close to the land, he smelled it. Sour, acrid, burning to the nostrils.

But Ernest was determined. He parked his car and went straight into the house. He hugged his mom and dad and asked if they'd take a walk with him down to the river. They were thrilled to have their son home again! Of course they'd take a walk.

He sat there on the rocks for a long time with the two of them. He poured out his heart and told them all he had learned about his own stinky feet. And to the surprise of one 19-year-old, two parents 48 and 50 years old peeled off socks and shoes and stuck their feet out in front of a young footwasher, saying, "Scrub away, son, scrub away."

Ernest's hands were shaking, just like the day he washed the old man's feet outside the diner. He pulled out the soaps, lotions and powders and untied a towel from around his waist. His parents talked about the years of neglect and pride and stubbornness as their son gently soaked, bathed, lotioned and powdered their feet. "Please forgive us," came the words in a whisper and a sniffle. "Oh, son, please forgive us."

The moon was full that night and a crispy, cold wind had begun to blow at that very moment of confession, sending the smell of The Land of Stinky Feet right back into their noses. It was awful! Worse than ever before! It kind of got stuck in your nose and throat when you breathed and it burned.

"Ohhh, hard to believe we couldn't smell that before."

"That's the problem with stinky feet, Mom. A person doesn't always know they have 'em!"

Ernest helped his parents to their feet. They hugged for a very long time, a hug that said a thousand words.

"Well, what's next, son?" They were done and yet they were beginning again.

"Well, Dad, we each go find a pair of feet to wash."

And turning around, they began to climb up the rocks to the bank of the river. But their confessions of stinky feet had been carried along with that pungent wind. And those who had ears to hear and a nose to smell remembered the gentle Footwasher and the river.

Once they reached the clearing above the river bed they heard familiar voices and approaching feet.

"Grandpa Duncan, is that you?"

"Yes, indeedy it's me! Whew! Probably smelled me coming. Oh, Ernest, I need my feet washed. Grandma Duncan couldn't make it all the way to the river. She's back there sitting, but I promised her I'd be back to wash her feet lickety-split!"

"How about ours?" said other familiar voices in that small crowd. It was Mr. and Mrs. Gray—dear friends of the family. Ernest's parents stepped into view.

"We'd be glad to wash your feet."

It was amazing! It was a miracle! They were coming in little groups of twos and threes. They carried dusty pans, dingy towels, soaps, lotions and powders long forgotten, but they were coming.

The winds of change were blowing in The Land of Stinky Feet. And they say the winds of change are blowing, still . . . . ♦

The Land Of
Now!

This story was written on my wedding anniversary (of all days!) many years ago. God held up one of His holy mirrors and gently beckoned me to look at myself. Here's what I saw, with thanks to Dr. Seuss.

I woke up the other day
in the Land of **Now**!
A slight nasal
high pitch from
a voice brought me 'round.
In walked my husband
in a gray three-piece suit.
All dressed and ready at 6:22.
"**Now**, get up! You're late! As late as can be.
Timmy's lost his shirt
and here's your coffee.

"We're ready, you're not,
what's the matter with you?
We've got places to go and things to do!
Now zip, **now** zoom, **now**
fly into those jeans.
I'm **now** late for work and I'm hungry!"
"Who was that man?"

I rolled over and yawned.
"Doesn't he know it's the crack of dawn?"

No sooner had I thought that
when a tiny-sized him
walked into my room from out of the den.
"Mommy," he said. Oh, I liked that sound.
"**N**ow get up, **n**ow zip, **n**ow
fly into those jeans.
I'm **n**ow late for school and yes, I'm hungry!
What's wrong with you, Mommy?
You're slow as a slug.
Get the lead out **n**ow
or I'll miss story time on the rug!"

I was up! I was out! I was into those jeans.
In a split second or two
I had made a **N**ow lunch
Full of packages, cans,
and recyclable boxed punch.
"Oh, goody, my favorites,"
that voice once again.
"**N**ow, let's scurry, Mommy, scurry.
We can do it, we can!
We'll get some McHurry's food
and eat in the van!"

So off we flew in our fast automobile
and proceeded to zip past

the other cars' wheels.
We were smart. We had two in our automobile.
So we entered quite quickly
and proceeded to wait
At least seconds ahead of the others at the gate.
And we waited and moved
and waited and moved
Which put us in such a mood,
A mood so crude that even McHurry's food
Couldn't change such a mood.
Finally, we arrived. Timmy kissed me goodbye
and handed me a list that said,
"Now, get these done by five!"
"What's this?" I said to my dear little one.
"It's your list of Nows.
Here's your kiss—gotta run."

I was left all alone
with a list full of Nows,
not later, when there's time, or
as soon as you get 'round.
"No, no, no," it screamed, "Now!"—
every single thing on that list
with this sick kind of whine
and slight nasal high pitch.
It compelled me, it scared me,
it threatened and dared me.
I gave in, I was helpless,
what else could I do?

I'd take care of those
Nows and I'd do it by two!

Something had clicked, I felt strange,
there was this gleam in my eye,
"Beep, beep, out of my way!"
became my modus operandi.
I dropped the dog at the vet,
picked up props for the set,
washed and waxed the whole car,
made a work lunch at Dupar's.
I found a gift and some cards
and was really quite thrift,
did some shopping, bill paying,
all was moving quite swift.
The Nows were disappearing
before my very eyes.
And then I went home and to my surprise
found more Nows piled high
to the top of the skies!
"No problem," I thought,
shirking off all the "laters."
I'll have this house ready,
plus the roast and potaters.
I zoomed through that house
to my team gave a whistle.
And away we all flew on the back of the Bissel™.
To the top of the attic,
to the bottom of the cellar,

the house had been sparkled
by a mere storyteller.
The house smelled delicious,
of course it was dinner—
roast, potatoes, carrots, peas
and dessert's "sure winner."

Off I flew in my car—
it was one hour before two—
Dropped some cleaning, picked up the dog,
got a cut and shampoo.
I had done it! I had done it!
All the *N*ows by two!
Only slightly exhausted, and needing a snooze.

I picked up my Timmy, it was now about three.
I was feeling so happy and full of great glee.
When all of a sudden,
I heard that same kind of pitch
And his words brought me low,
to the bottom of the ditch.
"Look Mommy, a list, you have to *n*ow look,
It was down on the floor,
right under this book.
Oh, Mommy, you'll *n*ow
have to zip, zoom and spark
If you want to get these *N*ows done
before it gets dark."

I looked in the mirror—that look—it was back.
"Now hand me that list
and hold on to your snack!
We're out of here, Timmy. Buckle up your seat!
We'll get these Nows done.
They will not defeat!"
Well, we were zipping and zooming
at at least hyper speed,
checking off every Now and taking the lead.
"You'll not get me, you Nows!
I can do all of this work!
'Cause I'm faster, I'm quicker,"
I yelled with a smirk.
I was huffing and puffing—
it was quarter to dinner.
Set the table, tossed the salad, frosted
the dessert's "sure winner!"

"Hi, honey, I'm home!" He's ten minutes late!
"What's for dinner, I'm starving,
mm-mmm, it smells great!"

I took a deep breath and greeted my dear,
For I was too tired to yell in his ear.
Then we ate very quickly,
in The Land of Now, cleared the table,
did the dishes in an hour, somehow.
It was now time for resting—
oh, now there's a good joke.

Picked up toys, bathed Timmy,
took my own little soak.
By *N*ow I was yawning and dragging around.
I was exhausted and tired,
I'd been beat to the ground.
"I'm going to bed. I'll see you at six."
Put my head on the pillow,
but my mind seemed to fix
On the things I had done on
that day in the *N*ow.
It was really revealing, how did I allow?

Timmy's books had laid silent
on top of his bed,
not one single page
had I stopped him and read.
The garden was beckoning
with blooming wild flowers.
No minute to stop out of all of my hours.
A neighbor had called just wanting to talk,
"I'm too busy. Next week, we'll walk?"
My stories had stayed in their files quite nicely;
I was too busy checking off *N*ows so precisely.
And David. Had I called him
just once to say, "Hi?"
No, I was too busy with my *N*ow operandi.
I had zipped, I had zoomed,
I had done every *N*ow,
my day should have measured up

to one, big, fat "Wow!"
But it didn't,
I couldn't find one thing important in it.
I was laying there feeling oh so sad in the dark,
when a still, quiet voice spoke into my heart.

'Tis a gift to be simple,

'tis a gift to be free,

'Tis a gift to come down

where we ought to be.

And when we find ourselves

in a place just right,

'Twill be in the Valley of

Love and Delight.*

I woke up the next day,
I'm quite happy to say,
In a Valley quite nice and not far away.
There are no Nows here,
unless I let them come near.
You see, I found out it's my choice
of the Voice that I'm going to hear. ♦

*From the old Shaker hymn "Simple Gifts"

Ralph
Twigger,
InnKeeper

Ralph Twigger—what
fun I'm having writing
stories about everyone's
favorite senior citizen!
May this Everyman
speak to your heart
about feeling important,
needed, and loved.

Ralph Twigger had been caring for Debra's two boys, Josh and Jeremy, since March. He saw them off to school in the morning, helped with homework in the afternoon—all in exchange for a home-cooked meal. There had been a few adventures. A man in his seventies is bound to forget a few lunches. Then there was the end of the year party when Ralph served as a "Room Mom" for both boys' classes. No one would ever forget Ralph's Peanut Butter Surprise cookies.

They were enjoying holidays just like a family. The fourth of July was a picnic in the park with fireworks. Halloween was a hoot when all four of them dressed up as crayons. Thanksgiving was real nice, too, with lots more to be thankful for than just Swanson's Frozen Dinners.

But right after the Thanksgiving meal, the

boys pulled out coloring books, crayons, construction paper, glue and glitter. Ralph soon figured it out: a ritual to usher in the Christmas season had descended upon this home. They'd barely finished the pumpkin pie when the Christmas carols began flowing.

"Help us, Ralph!" Josh, the oldest, was great at getting Ralph to try anything once.

"No, thank you. I'm no artist." Ralph was starting to feel a sad ache in the pit of his stomach that he hadn't felt for a long time. He did not enjoy Christmas. He had stopped celebrating it when his wife, Rachel, died.

"Please, Ralph. Mom got you a Christmas coloring book and crayons, too!" Jeremy held them up for display.

"What?!"

Debra giggled as she handed him a cup of eggnog. Ralph hated eggnog, but politely took a sip. "It was the boys' idea. They said you like to color."

He swallowed the funny-tasting concoction, trying not to breathe. "Well now, that's because the boys need some help from time to time with their coloring assignments." He sounded a bit angry and the boys picked that up in his voice quickly.

"What's wrong, Ralph?"

The clock was sounding the hour of nine and his excuse for leaving this pre-Christmas celebration.

"I think we've worn Ralph out, boys."

"I am a little tired," he said, relieved that he had an excuse for his premature exit. As he walked over to the door, Debra met him there with an armload of leftovers.

"Here you go." She hugged him and whispered in his ear, "Thank you, Ralph, for all you've been to me and the boys. We love you."

His tongue stuck to the roof of his mouth. That sad feeling was there.

"Bye. See you tomorrow, Ralph." Jeremy and Josh were waving the paper chain.

He knew he was about to cry. He couldn't even say good night. In seconds he was back in his apartment. He slammed the plastic containers of leftovers on the counter. "Rachel, Rachel, I can't do this without you!" He muffled the loudness of his voice with his hand.

This was her time of year. Rachel was so alive at Christmas. She loved everything about it. Their home looked like a Christmas card. Perfectly wrapped packages spilled out from under a tree that looked like snow had fallen on it.

Gingerbread men marched in and out of the branches among hundreds of German hand-blown glass ornaments. Rachel dragged him to every Christmas event the city offered, except church. He always found a way to wiggle out of religious programs. Christmas Eve was the hardest. "Is there room in the Inn, Ralph?" She never pushed her beliefs. And sadly, Ralph never accepted them.

"No," he'd say in too stern a voice. "There's no room in the Inn." Then, an uncomfortable lump would rise in his throat as Rachel headed to church, unaccompanied every Christmas Eve. After she left, he felt so alone, so separate from her. Now that same old uncomfortable feeling was back. But this time it lay in the pit of his stomach. How was he going to get through this Christmas?

No one gets a tree this early! He peeked out the window as Debra and the boys dragged the tree up the apartment stairwell. He'd refused to go with them, but he had to help now. They were about to fall down the stairway with the thing.

"Oh, Ralph, thank you. Isn't she a beauty?"

Ralph had heard Rachel use those very words for more than forty years.

Silently, he helped with the stand. The boys wanted the tree in their room, but agreed that the best place for it was in front of the living room window.

"Everyone will see it!" said Jeremy.

"Great. Everyone." For the next month, Ralph would see this tree every day as he cared for the boys. And by the looks of all the boxes of decorations, the entire apartment would be transformed by mid-afternoon.

"How about lunch and some tree trimming, Ralph?" Debra could make scrubbing floors sound exciting, but not this—not trimming a tree.

"Please!" The boys were begging in a way that he had such a hard time refusing.

"I've got repairs waiting for me, but thank you for asking." He was proud of himself. He'd managed a polite response. *It's going to take days to get the sap off my hands.*

Thanksgiving passed and the boys returned to school. But every day brought more invitations:

"How about some Christmas shopping?"

"I don't buy presents. I send money orders."

"Want to come caroling?"

"I'm too old to carol!"

"We're baking Christmas cookies."

"Gotta watch my sugar intake."

"Ice skating?"

"Are you kidding?"

He was cranky and short with the boys. He even refused to go to their school Christmas pageant. It was confusing to Josh and Jeremy, but they loved Ralph. Finally, the boys decided that when school let out for Christmas vacation, they would confront Ralph. "We're gonna find out why Ralph hates Christmas."

The boys were quiet that morning and so was Ralph. He received no invitations to any Christmas falderal, which suited Ralph just fine. After school, two boys knocked on Ralph's door at ten minutes after three o'clock bearing tissue-wrapped clay creations.

"You can open 'em, Ralph," said Josh in a monotone.

"You sure? Isn't there a rule against early present opening?"

"Nah, go ahead. You might as well." Jeremy sounded so sad.

Caught off guard, Ralph opened the gifts. "Oh, boys, these are very nice."

"It's a dinosaur," said Josh.

"And a little bowl you can use for tiny watch parts or paper clips," said Jeremy.

That lump was back in his throat and his stomach churned. He wanted to throw his arms around the boys and tell them that these gifts were the finest presents he'd ever received. Instead, he sat there and mumbled, "Thank you."

The boys looked at each other and Josh elbowed Jeremy. It was time.

"Ralph, we have something very serious to ask you."

"All right, I'm ready."

"How come you hate Christmas?" Two little cherub faces stared at him. He couldn't tell these boys the truth. They were too young to understand death and disappointment.

"Now, come on, guys. I'm no worse than Ebeneezer Scrooge or that green fellow in Dr. Seuss' . . . ."

"The Grinch," they both chimed.

"Yes, the Grinch or . . . or . . . the Innkeeper in the Christmas story? Tell me, am I?" His mean voice was back.

There was a long pause—uncomfortably long for Ralph.

"I'm sorry I have to say this, Ralph," said

Josh calmly. "But you're just like Scrooge and the Grinch."

There was a little pause in the list. "And the Innkeeper?"

The boys gave a resounding, "Yes!"

"You have no room for Christmas in your heart," added Jeremy.

The indictment was delivered by two tiny messengers. Guilty. It was one of those rare moments of truth when a person has an opportunity of a lifetime to change.

But Ralph sat there numb. Speechless. Stomach churning. Finally, he went to the kitchen and poured a glass of chocolate milk. "Would you like some chocolate milk?" The boys shook their heads no. He returned to some work while the boys colored. In silence, they made a Christmas card for Ralph which they stuck in the refrigerator next to the chocolate milk.

It was five o'clock. Debra was home now. The boys gathered their backpacks and headed next door. Ralph heard the door shut and reached for the phone.

"Oh, hi Ralph." There was a long pause before Debra spoke again. "I see. We'll miss you. You take care and have a good weekend. The boys will see you on Monday. Bye."

Ralph knew this was the best thing. Although he'd miss Debra's cooking this weekend, he needed a break from the boys and they needed a break from him. He stood up and felt a little queasy. *Wonder if that chocolate milk was sour?* He definitely felt a dull headache, too. Ralph opened the fridge and found the card leaning against the milk carton. In a child's scrawl, it read, "Merry Christmas, Ralph. We love you. Jeremy and Josh."

Grabbing the card, a carton of orange juice and a box of Ritz crackers, Ralph headed for bed. He ate crackers, drank orange juice and watched the news. Then it started—a sneezing attack, from out of nowhere. Fortunately, he had a box of tissues nearby. He sneezed and sneezed until his ears popped and his head pounded.

"I think I'm sick," Ralph moaned as he searched the bathroom cabinet for cold medicine and a thermometer. He was sick all right. *It's just a twenty-four-hour bug. I'll be fine by Monday.* But he wasn't fine. In fact, he was delirious with fever. At eight o'clock the boys knocked and rang the doorbell. But they couldn't raise Ralph.

"What do we do, Josh, call the police?"

"No. Maybe Ralph ran an errand and got stuck somewhere. We'll give him twenty minutes."

The boys stared at Ralph's apartment door as Josh's watch ticked off the minutes. Then they pounded on the door and rang the bell over and over again. In a moment of consciousness, Ralph called their names, faintly.

"What was that?" said Josh.

Jeremy's ear was pressed against the door like Josh's. "What? I didn't hear anything."

"I thought I heard Ralph's voice."

"Maybe he's hurt!"

The boys ran back to their apartment and called their mom at work. She was home in ten minutes. They used the extra key Ralph had given them and found him, burning with fever.

"Rachel, Rachel. I'm sorry."

"Rest now," Debra said, feeling his forehead. "You're very sick, Ralph."

"Mom, why is he calling you Rachel? She's dead."

"It's the fever, boys. Get me some wet washcloths and I'll call the doctor."

✻✖✖✖✻

Ralph recovered fully in a few days. He was a bit embarrassed, but grateful to the boys and Debra for nursing him back to health. How could he thank them?

He began pulling out boxes that had been hidden away for years. One was marked "train set." *Yes, those boys are gonna have a train for that tree.* He dug through the box marked "tree," pulling out carefully wrapped ornaments for Debra. *She'll love these.* Then he saw it: a present. On the tag, Rachel had written, "To my husband of 43 years. Love, Rachel." His hands trembled and the heavy feeling in his stomach was back. Ralph untied the ribbon and opened the box. Inside was a pocket watch he had admired and a fine gold fob chain. Inscribed on the inside were the words, "Is there room in the Inn?"

Ralph was overcome with the beauty of the gift and the words Rachel had left behind. He sobbed and hugged the watch close to his heart. Rachel had found her way into this old heart. So had those little boys and their mother, but never Jesus.

"There are so many things I regret. I'm too mean and bitter and old to let Him in. How do you let in Someone you've spent your life ignoring? I don't know how." He paused, groping for words he'd never said before. "I don't know how to let You in."

There was no one else in the apartment at the time. But, clear as a bell, he heard the gentle answer: "Ask me in, Ralph."

Ralph showered, shaved, and dressed in his bow tie and a new sweater from his sister. The watch fob gleamed below his sweater band. He knocked on the apartment door and held out two packages in grand presentation.

The door opened and Ralph said the words, "Is there room in the Inn?"

The boys tackled him as Debra giggled with delight at Ralph's polished appearance. There was a twinkle in his eyes she'd never seen before. She hugged this dear man who had become like a father to her. "There is always room for Ralph Twigger."

Rachel would have loved the next scene. There was Ralph, sitting in church on Christmas Eve, sandwiched between two little boys and their mother. Beaming from ear to ear, he sang at the top of his voice, "Joy to the world, the Lord is come."

And He had come . . . and made His home in Ralph Twigger's heart. ♦

The King Who Waits

My first oral story—
written to encourage
college students in their
search for a personal
relationship with God.
May it do the same
for you.

There is a King, unlike any other king you've read about in history books or fairy tales. A king far too wonderful to ever be compared to any of these kinds of kings. For this Great King does not seek power or rule, but relationship with all of His subjects. And to each subject that seeks Him earnestly, he or she becomes an heir to all the great and wonderful treasures the King has been storing away for them since the beginning of time.

By now, you might be wondering, "What does this King want in return for all of that?" I have stumbled through my life over that very question. Stumbled and stumbled. But last night I learned the answer. All this Great King wants in return is this: just that we come.

Every day, the Great King, long before His subjects have risen, begins a morning ritual of preparation. All the windows are thrust open to let in the scents of early morning; the marble entry way is washed, waxed, polished to a brilliant shine; the meals for the day are prepared; fresh flowers are cut and placed in all the rooms and the library is carefully inspected to be sure that all is ready for Him and His subjects.

The library is my favorite room in the King's mansion and I believe that if He had to choose just one room, this would be His favorite too. It holds a specialness for many reasons. The pictures of His subjects that line the piano, the trinkets many have given Him scattered here and there. The huge, stone fireplace with its two worn out, but comfortable overstuffed chairs. Three of the four walls are lined with books from floor to ceiling. The fourth wall has this enormous picture window, complete with dreamy landscape. I tell you, it's the kind of room you'd want to spend the day in—willingly, gladly.

Maybe that's why the Great King is always there when I come. He's always there, sitting in one of the overstuffed chairs. And never has a day passed when I've not been offered a brownie, a raspberry tart, even a meal in his beautifully tiled kitchen. There seems to be no end to His care and concern for me. Such a loving King.

Yet, I can't remember the last time I stayed longer than ten or fifteen minutes or met his greeting with the same warmth. You see, I am one of His subjects who has always kept Him waiting, wondering whether I'd ever show up at all and always in a hurry. But not today. Last night changed my reason for going forever!

You see, last night I dropped by for only a few minutes. I told the Great King, "I've been running around for everyone else today and tonight dear King, tonight it's time for me." As I was babbling on, I noticed the King began to draw away. He began to share about His day. The King had never done this before. He said He had cleaned, prepared everything and finally sat back in one of the overstuffed chairs, ready for the first subjects who would be dropping by before work, school, the busyness of life. "Hour upon hour passed," He said. "And no one came by."

He forgave them, just the same, and continued to wait and wait and wait. And as He waited, He began to daydream about His subjects. When they first met Him, how they'd grown, all their special times together. He said he had thought of me that day. Of course, I was very touched. He said He had remembered, among all the times we'd shared, this past spring. How depressed and alone I'd felt. His smiling eyes affirmed my memory. "Remember," He said, "We spent the day together?" I assured the King that I did remember that day. I remember, I left His mansion feeling better than I had felt in months.

His eyes were different now. "I waited for you." His words were not condemning me. "I waited for you to return and tell me things were better. I waited weeks without a word from you."

Well, I was beginning to feel that gnawing, almost sick feeling in the stomach. The kind that comes when a dear friend confronts a hurt.

The striking of noon had brought the King back to the present and still, no one had come. Once again, the Great King forgave them and headed off to the kitchen to prepare the noon meal. "One of the loneliest sandwiches I'd eaten in a long time," he added to the telling.

He was clearing the sandwiches away, brushing the crumbs from His place when an overwhelming sadness swept over Him and He dropped to the cold floor and began to weep. "I want them. I want them. Oh, how I want them. When will they understand?"

After a bit, the Great King pulled Himself up from that cold floor, patted dry the tears, brushed off His robes, and went back to the library to wait for the first subject.

It was me. I was that first subject. And as He opened the doors, I didn't notice the tear-stained cheeks, the hands outstretched to embrace me as never before. I hadn't noticed any of that. In fact, it wasn't until I sat down with Him, face to face, at that small wooden table and heard those words, "I want them," was served one more meal by my Great King, and again, "I simply want them." It wasn't until then that I realized: the Great King wants me! The Great King wants me!

We talked and talked late into the night. We had brownies and raspberry tarts far too late, but we had the best time I remember spending in all our times together. It was very late when I left his mansion. But that night I took a step closer to Him. A step I could have taken long ago in my life. A step I never had time for until yesterday.

And today will be different. Today, I will spend time with my King. Today I will give more than I think I can spare. And today, I'm going to listen, instead of always asking and wanting and talking. He has so much to offer me. So much to offer you. The Great King who waits has waited long enough for this subject. ♦

How
this Book
Came to
Be

In a land not far away from the heart there lived a writer and storyteller who wanted more than anything to share her stories with others . . . on paper, bound and about the size of a lunch bag, purse, Bible or daily calendar.

In her land there also lived two very good friends who wanted to help her produce this book of stories. One friend was an editor and, oh how she could chop, snip and tuck a story. And the other friend was quite magical upon the keyboard and could make a story look wonderful on a page.

Every Tuesday for what seemed like months, these two friends and the writer and storyteller gathered to work at the stories. They worked and worked and laughed and laughed. And drank too much coffee and ate too much chocolate.

About six o'clock, though, every Tuesday, they would cease their labor.

They, and their husbands and children, would all sit down to a feast and they all would eat dinner together—all nine of them and one dog. And they would, of course, laugh and drink too much coffee. Then their husbands and all of the children would go home to bed. And the friends would once again work on the stories of the writer and storyteller until they got punchy and silly. This was always a good sign that they were done for the night.

And then, after what really seemed like months, it was finished. All the stories were put into a big box and sent to a special publisher. After many months it came back with a note that said something like, "Thank you, but no thank you."

Well, this blow should have defeated these three friends. All that time, all that coffee, all that chocolate. But they gathered up all the stories of the writer and storyteller and they developed another plan. "We will send it to other lands and other publishers!" They did.

But alas, after many months all of the notes came back.

This time, the notes were even nicer. "Thank you. This shows promise."

Did this stop these three friends? No. "We will break the book down," they said. "And we will send out the best story!" They did. It was a very special story the writer and storyteller had written about God. It always made all three of them cry and they had heard it and read it many, many times. "This story is the one," they all agreed.

But alas after many months all of the notes came back once again.

This time, the notes were stronger. "Good story. But we have no place for it."

Did this stop these three friends? No. They put their heads together along with some other special people who really liked the first book idea—a collection of stories. They told the writer and storyteller to create a book. They said, "Take six of your best stories and call it *Right-Side-Up Stories For Upside-Down People.* That has always been a good title!"

And the three friends, plus others, were very happy.

And so it came to pass in a land not far away from the heart . . . and here it is in your hands.

That's my story. That's the story of how this book came to be. I think it is good to know the story of how books are created. They are made with lots of thought and creativity and many relationships. Books do not happen without people. And so I want to thank the people who have helped to create this first volume of *Right-Side-Up Stories For Upside-Down People*.

My two dear friends, Marcia Coppess and Vicki Reese—my Editor and Typographer. You two have been here from the very beginning. Thank you for believing in me and working so hard to make this book happen. Coffee and chocolate will always taste better with you!

George Baldwin, who coordinated and led and encouraged us through the book process. Thank you for your wisdom at every turn.

Karen Newe, for the beauty of her artwork and shaping of the book upon the pages. Oh, Karen! We started talking about a someday book when we first met. Remember?

My Right-Side-Up Stories board for believing in this book and giving us an extra push! You are the best Gary, George, Annie, Steve, Vicki, Marcia, Michael, Prudence, Bob, Esther and Brian.

My prayer team who cared for you, the

reader, long before you ever picked up this book to read it. Thank you, my dear brothers and sisters, for all you've given to us in prayer.

My mentors and models—Grandma Lucy, Grandpa Herb, Grandma Bess, Mom and Dad, Margie, Michael and Melanee, Aunt Betty, Uncle Frank and Aunt Lois, Aunt Mary, Uncle Bob and Aunt Eva, Mrs. Blackwood, Mr. Huscroft, Mrs. Cooney, Ray Rood, Tim Purga, Andrea McAleenan, John Wallace, Cora Alley, Gary Tiffin, H.B. London, Jr., Kathy and Ed Long, Margie and Dick Coffin, Lois Sowers, Sharon Densford, Mark Sanford, Prudence Dancy, Perry Moore, Gary Bayer and David. I was always watching. I am still watching. Thank you.

David, my husband, who always seeks God's best for me and our ministry of Right-Side-Up Stories. You are my dear gift from God. You are my most beloved story.

Timothy, my son, who practically writes every Ralph Twigger story with me! You, my dear gift from God, are the reason I love story. You give me a reason to write and tell to children and adults. May these stories always lead you back to Him.

To my Heavenly Father, the Author of all Life! Thank you for allowing me to write and tell stories. Thank you for allowing me the honor of being used.

About
Melea J. Brock
& Right-Side-Up
Stories

Melea J. Brock writes and tells stories for the Child inside everyone—from the swaggering youth trying desperately to convince us—and himself—that he's all grown up, to the elder in our midst whose age might cause us to expect her to have all the answers. Each of us—busy office worker, over-committed mom, distracted college student and electronic age child—has a place deep within that responds to Melea's stories and storytelling.

Trained in social work and drama, Melea began writing stories to communicate difficult truths to college students with whom she worked.

Since 1982, her stories have taken her across the United States and into Canada telling to audiences that have varied from several thousand people to intimate settings such as family rooms and the side of hospital beds. Her original stories and folktales have been produced in more than half a dozen cassette tapes and numerous magazines.

In addition to storyteller and writer, Melea boasts of more creative form in the roles of wife and mom. Her husband, David, and son, Timothy, make their home in an old 1922 farmhouse in La Crescenta, California.

As always, she welcomes your response, comments and questions. Permission for story use can be sought at this address:

Melea J. Brock
Right-Side-Up Stories
260 S. Lake Avenue, #185
Pasadena, CA 91101
(800) 369-9230
e-mail: astory4u@earthlink.net

The stories in this book appear on the following story tapes:

Step Inside, Volume 2
Mary Alice Bennett's Box, Volume 3
The Worriers, Volume 5
The Land of Stinky Feet, Volume 2
The Land of Now!, Volume 2
Ralph Twigger, Innkeeper, Volume 4
The King Who Waits, Volume 3